To my son MAC - Don't be afraid to be you!
- LG3

Please visit us at
visionquestkids.com

FIRST EDITION

2 4 6 8 10 9 7 5 3 1

Library of Congress Cataloging-in-Publication Data

Goss, Leon, 1966-
    Selfus Esteemus Personalitus Low / by Leon Goss III ; illustrated by
Ken Tunell. -- 1st ed.
        p. cm.
    Summary: When Copernicus Worrious is diagnosed with "Selfus
Esteemus Personalitus Low," his doctor prescribes a special cure.
    ISBN-13: 978-1-933156-00-2 (hardcover : alk. paper)
    ISBN-13: 978-1-933156-08-8 (pbk. : alk. paper)
    [1. Self-esteem--Fiction. 2. Self-perception--Fiction. 3. Stories in
rhyme.]   I. Tunell, Ken, ill. II. Title.
PZ8.3.G674Sel 2005
[E]--dc22
                                                    2005018835

Selfus Esteemus Personalitus Low

By Leon Goss III

Illustrated by Ken Tunell

Copernicus Worrious

Is a sad single son
who DOESN'T know how to just play and have fun.
He always wants to hit a home run,
slam dunk the ball and be number one.

But of course, that is never the way it can be.
And as hard as he tries, he can't quite see
Why he ends up feeling exactly the same,
No matter if winning or losing the game.

"I feel like a loser, a no-name, a chump.
I feel that I'm lower than the lowest stump.
And no matter how many successes I see,
I'm thinking that everyone's laughing at me."

Yet somehow he knew that he had to get help.
So he went straight to a doctor who knew how he felt.

Dr. Artemis Pessimist rose from his chair.
--Very tall and odd, from his socks to his hair.

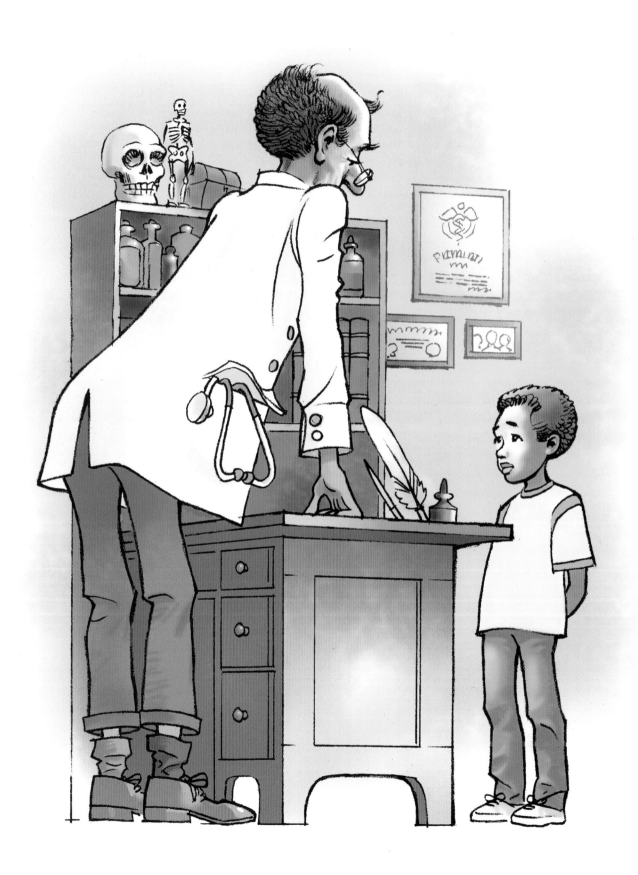

The sign on his door read, 'A Doctor of Doubt,'
but as he offered his chair his kindness stood out.

"Let me look in your ears.
Bend your knees till they meet."

"Stand on one leg. Touch your nose and your feet.
Now, kindly describe every morsel you eat."

They talked for a while, then the good doctor said,
"Aha! I know what's going on in your head."

"You're feeling quite worthless and that makes you hurt.
You think you're a failure and your friends think you're dirt."

"That's right!" said Copernicus, "How did you know?"
The doctor said, "It's a disease we outgrow.
I know how you feel because I had it too.
It's hard to detect 'cause it's just like the flu.
It's a common condition. I must let you know...
you have   Selfus Esteemus
Personalitus
Low."

"Selfus Esteemus Personalitus Low,"
repeated Copernicus many times, very slow.

"Oh no!" said the boy with a bit of alarm,
"Will you give me some pills or a shot in my arm?"

"Well," said the doctor, "If you will agree,
You can have the same cure that my doctor gave me."

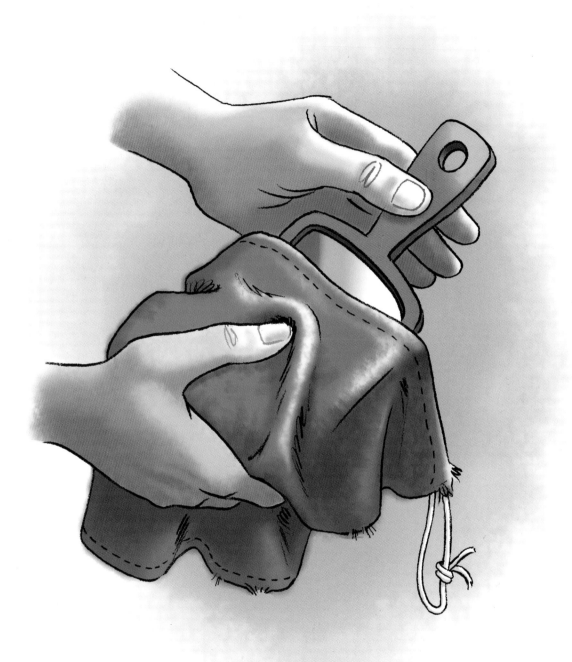

Dr. Pessimist pulled out a blue velvet bag.
It was tattered and faded and looked like a rag.
--Lay a mirror inside that the good doctor drew,
Then he said to Copernicus, "This will help you."

"And yes," said the doctor, "This is a fact."
"If you ignore the condition it might lead to an attack
    of the contagious **Queenus Dramaticus Flu.**"

Copernicus squealed,

"Doctor, What should I do?"

"You'll know that you
have it, if your nose
turns beet red..."

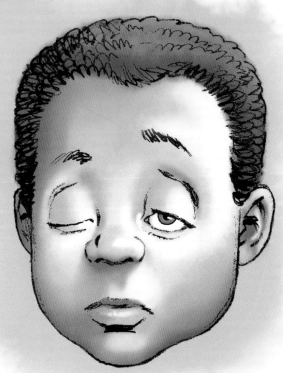

"...and your eyes
almost drop down out
of your head."

Then Dr. Pessimist looked him straight in the eye
and explained what to do with an earnest reply,

"You must follow a regimen, twice, everyday.
You must look at yourself in this mirror and say,

I am worthy of you, I know this is true
and I don't really care what others may do."

"Now Copernicus," said the doctor,
"Disease Eradicus, which is the cure to it all,
Will start right away when you let your guard fall.
Stop judging yourself like you think others do.
You must be your own champion and cheerleader too."

The good doctor sent the young boy on his way,
With the mirror in hand...to be used everyday.

A short while from the doctor, just one block or two,
Copernicus passed by a man with one shoe.
This man had a bird on his head. Yes it's true.
And he wore one sock red and the other one blue.

Then abruptly, the man said,
"How do you do?"
and did you know
that your nose
is as **red** as
my shoe?

Then the man said goodbye and quickly departed,
While Copernicus thought that the fever had started.

He remembered the mirror as he took it in hand
And repeated the words at the doctor's command...

"I am worthy of you, I know this is true
and I don't really care what others may do."

He nervously looked at his mirrored reflection.
Afraid that he'd see the red imperfection.

But he felt so relieved
when he finally did see...

As natural and healthy a nose as could be!

Copernicus continued on his way home,
Until he met with a woman who sat all alone.

Her left and right stockings were bunched at her knees
and she screeched out a delicate tune as she pleased.

She stood on her feet and said, "Pardon me sir,
But your eyes are as droopy as Shar-Pei dog fur."
Then she curtsied to him and went off on her way,
Leaving Copernicus in utter dismay.

Copernicus was now very anxious to know
If the flu had progressed. Yes, the mirror would show.
But one look confirmed what he thought he might see.
"The healthiest Copernicus staring at me!"

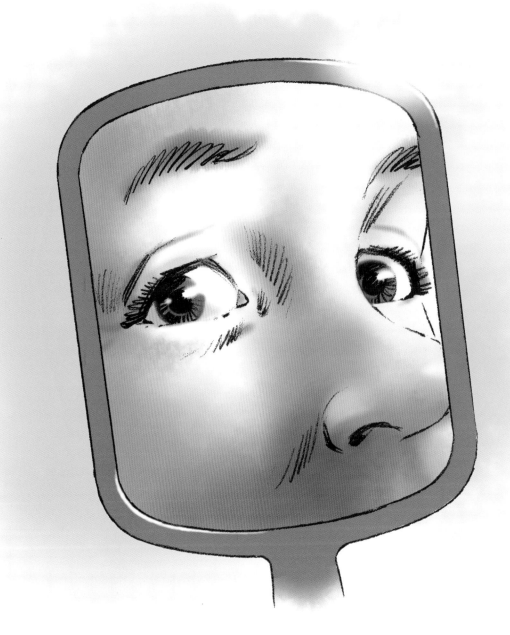

"And my eyes are not heavy or droopy at all
And I didn't have to recite or recall

I am worthy of you, I know this is true
and I don't really care what others may do."

So Copernicus went out to play with his friends.
And he didn't care if he'd lose or he'd win.

He just wanted to play and to have lots of fun
And to jump and to kick and to run in the sun.

And no matter who laughed when he took a big fall,
Copernicus Worrious was having a ball.

Now Copernicus thought, "I feel good about me
And things are not always that bad. I can see."

Then he placed the small mirror upon a near shelf,
So that when he was sad he could say to himself,

"I am worthy of you, I know this is true
and I don't really care what others may do."

The young boy felt better, all in one day.
He recalled the strange people he met on the way.
Yet Copernicus thought of a curious fact.
Dr. Pessimist's socks were never exact.

They slouched, they were BUNCHED and were oftentimes Patched.

And the funny thing is they were always mismatched.

But no matter, he was cured of his ailment; and so,
Copernicus Worrious no longer suffered from
Selfus Esteemus Personalitus Low.